WHAT COLOR WAS THE SKY TODAY?

BY **MIELA FORD**

PICTURES BY **SALLY NOLL**

GREENWILLOW BOOKS, NEW YORK

For Bob
—M. F.

For S. N. and M. N.
—S. N.

Gouache paints were used for the full-color art.
The text type is Swiss 721.

Text copyright © 1997 by Miela Ford
Illustrations copyright © 1997 by Sally Noll
All rights reserved. No part of this book may be
reproduced or utilized in any form or by any
means, electronic or mechanical, including
photocopying, recording, or by any information
storage and retrieval system, without permission
in writing from the Publisher, Greenwillow Books,
a division of William Morrow & Company, Inc.,
1350 Avenue of the Americas,
New York, NY 10019.

Printed in Hong Kong by South China
Printing Company (1988) Ltd.

First Edition 10 9 8 7 6 5 4 3 2 1

Library of Congress Cataloging-in-Publication Data

Ford, Miela.
What color was the sky today? / by Miela Ford ;
pictures by Sally Noll.
       p.   cm.
Summary: Illustrates the different colors that
can appear in the sky as the weather changes
during the day.
ISBN 0-688-14558-2 (trade)
ISBN 0-688-14559-0 (lib. bdg.)
[1. Sky—Fiction.   2. Color—Fiction.]
I. Noll, Sally, ill.   II. Title.
PZ7.F75322Wh   1997
[E]—dc20   96-10413
CIP   AC

Sunrise.
The day begins.

The sun starts to climb.

Little white clouds
stretch across the sky.

Can you count them?

More clouds come.
Now they are gray.
Will they hide the sun?

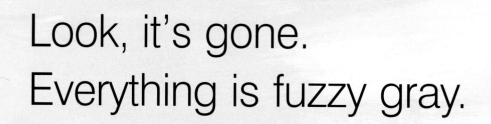

Look, it's gone.
Everything is fuzzy gray.

Raindrops
hit the ground.
*Plink, plunk,
splat,* and *splash.*

Then it's quiet.
Look up! A little blue
is peeking through.

The sun is back.
And there's a rainbow!
Red, orange, yellow, green,
blue, indigo, and violet.

Look carefully.
Rainbows don't last long.

Sunset.
The day ends.

What color was
the sky today?

Can you remember?